THE
FORTUNE·TELLERS

THE FORTUNE·TELLERS

BY LLOYD ALEXANDER

ILLUSTRATED BY TRINA SCHART HYMAN

DUTTON CHILDREN'S BOOKS   NEW YORK

Un petit cadeau pour Michou
de la mère de sa mère, T.S.H.,
et du plus vieux de ses amis
nouveaux, L.A.

Text copyright © 1992 by Lloyd Alexander
Illustrations copyright © 1992 by Trina Schart Hyman

Library of Congress Cataloging-in-Publication Data
Alexander, Lloyd.
The fortune-tellers/by Lloyd Alexander;
illustrated by Trina Schart Hyman. —1st ed.
p.   cm.
Summary: A carpenter goes to a fortune-teller and finds the
predictions about his future come true in an unusual way.
ISBN 0-525-44849-7
[1. Fortune-telling—Fiction.   2. Humorous stories.]
I. Hyman, Trina Schart, ill.   II. Title.
PZ7.A3774Fn   1992
[E]—dc20   91-30684   CIP   AC

Published in the United States by Dutton Children's Books,
a division of Penguin Books USA Inc.
375 Hudson Street, New York, New York 10014
Editor: Ann Durell   Designer: Riki Levinson
Printed in the U.S.A.
First Edition   10 9 8 7 6 5 4 3 2

The full-color illustrations, a combination of ink, acrylic,
and crayon, are painted on Arches watercolor board.

A young carpenter was unhappy in his trade. "Will I be hammering and sawing the rest of my days?" he asked himself. "Without wife or sweetheart? And nothing but long labor for little pay?"

He kept wondering if the future held anything better.

Hearing that a fortune-teller had come to the neighboring town, he set off eagerly to learn the answers to his questions. He found the prophet living in a room above a cloth merchant's shop.

"My first prediction is this," the fortune-teller said before the carpenter could begin. "You're going to pay me a nice fee. But that's a mere trifle to someone destined for wealth."

"Do you see me rich, then?" exclaimed the carpenter, gladly handing over the coins the fortune-teller demanded.

"Rich you will surely be," answered the fortune-teller, settling his magic cap on his head and gazing into the crystal ball on the table. "On one condition: that you earn large sums of money."

"Marvelous!" cried the carpenter. "Things look brighter already. And with so much wealth—will I be famous, too?"

"No question about it," said the fortune-teller, "once you become well known."

"Amazing!" said the carpenter. "But, now, tell me: Will I marry and be happy ever after?"

"You shall wed your true love," said the fortune-teller, "if you find her and she agrees. And you shall be happy as any in the world if you can avoid being miserable."

"Better and better!" said the carpenter. "And shall we have a long life together?"

"The longest," replied the fortune-teller, again peering into the crystal ball. "Only one thing might cut it short: an early demise."

"Wonderful!" cried the carpenter. "Thank you, master seer, thank you."

With that, he left the fortune-teller and hurried homeward, impatient for all these good things to happen.

He had scarcely gone halfway when he thought of a dozen more questions he was burning to ask. So he turned around and ran back as fast as he could.

To his surprise and disappointment, he found the room empty. The fortune-teller's cap and crystal ball were on the table.

Puzzling over what had become of their owner, the carpenter ventured to pick up the objects, eyeing them with fear and fascination.

As he did, the door flew open and in stormed the cloth merchant's wife. She stopped in her tracks, and her eyes popped in astonishment.

"A miracle!" she burst out. "Only this morning you were a scruffy old codger. You've changed yourself into a handsome young man!

"What powers you have," she went on. "To think I took you for a fraud and was coming to throw you out of the house. Honored guest! Stay as long as you like. I'll never ask a penny's rent if you'll tell our fortunes."

The carpenter tried to explain, but the cloth merchant's wife would hear none of it. She called in her husband and daughter. They all insisted so firmly that the carpenter at last put on the cap, sat down at the table, and peered into the crystal ball.

"Tell me straight off," said the cloth merchant's wife. "Are we to be rich? With fine clothes, horses, and herds of cattle?"

Though he stared and squinted, the bewildered carpenter saw nothing whatever. At a loss for what else to do, he recalled what the fortune-teller had told him.

"Yes, enormously rich," said the carpenter, "as soon as you gain a lot of money. You'll have all those good things once you can afford to buy them."

"Shall we live long and happy?" asked the cloth merchant.

"Indeed so," replied the carpenter. "You need only stay healthy and keep breathing."

"And I?" asked the cloth merchant's daughter. "Shall I find my true love?"

"Ah—as for that," said the carpenter, blushing a little, "I can assure you it will happen. In fact, it's happened already."

Hearing of this marvelous prophet, the neighbors came clamoring to know their futures, pressing coins into the hands of the carpenter, who told the same to each in turn.

"If that's all there is to it," he said to himself, "I like it better than carpentry."

So, instead of going back to his hammer and saw, he set up as a fortune-teller.

His fame spread quickly. He grew richer than he had ever dreamed, married the cloth merchant's daughter, and lived long years of happiness.

As to the real fortune-teller:

While he had been leaning over the balcony, wondering if tomorrow would be hotter than yesterday, he lost his balance, tumbled down into a passing cart, and jolted the driver off the seat.

The frightened ox bolted, went plunging through town into the savanna where the fortune-teller was thrown clear, only to be chased by a lion and, as he climbed a tree to escape, he broke open a hornet's nest and...

fighting off the angry swarm was snatched from the branch by a giant eagle who carried him aloft and dropped him into a river where he was swept downstream and never seen or heard from again.

Despite his wealth and fame, the carpenter never forgot his benefactor. Although in time he gave up wondering what had happened to the fortune-teller, the carpenter thought of him frequently with warmth and gratitude for having seen the future so clearly.